"Don't worry," Jonathan said. "We're the best."

Tommy walked Jonathan over to the mat. He gave him some instructions, then stepped back.

Jonathan bowed to his opponent. He was a thin boy in a black and white gi.

They both bowed to the judges.

The referee gave the start command. Jonathan felt his stomach jump.

The next thing that jumped was the boy.

He came at Jonathan all hands and feet.

Jonathan knew he didn't have a chance.

KARATE KIDS
Want to Win!

by **Alex Simmons**

illustrated by
Alan Tiegreen

created by
Steve DeMasco

This edition published in 2002.

Copyright © 1993 by Mega-Books of New York, Inc. and Stephen DeMasco.

Published by Troll Communications L.L.C.

ISBN 0-8167-7248-7

Printed in Canada.

10 9 8 7 6 5 4 3 2 1

TABLE OF CONTENTS

MEET THE KIDS
OF THE
COOL KARATE SCHOOL

Jonathan "Tiger" Scott
In karate, the Tiger stands for strength. In Jonathan's case, it also stands for stubborn and spoiled. Now Jonathan is learning that some things are more important than his parents' money.

Marissa "Dragon" Santos
The Dragon has fighting spirit. And so does Marissa. She says you have to have a fighting spirit with four older brothers. Not to mention a group of pushy friends.

Matthew "Snake" Davis
The Snake is quick and smooth. Being too smooth sometimes gets Matthew in trouble. He started studying karate to learn how to fight. Now he's learning a lot more than that.

Susan "Leopard" Ziegler
Fast and powerful, that's the Leopard. And so is Susan. Sometimes the leopard is angry—and so is Susan. The kids try to help, but she doesn't make it easy.

Willy "Crane" Ray
The Crane stands for grace and balance. Willy is tall and slim, like the crane. He's working on the grace and balance. He has to learn fast because his father is always pushing him to win.

CHAPTER

1

THE COOL
KARATE SCHOOL

"Get your smelly foot out of my face!" Willy Lee Ray said.

He was facing a girl with frizzy blond hair. She was pointing her bare foot at his chest.

"My feet are not smelly," Susan Ziegler said. She lowered her leg. "You're mad because you couldn't block that kick."

"Boy, I wish I had that on film." Jonathan Scott circled Willy and Susan. He was pretending to hold a movie camera. "That was really — "

"Graceful?" Susan asked.

"No. Funny-looking." Jonathan smiled.

"Thanks a heap," Willy mumbled.

Jonathan, Susan, and Willy were students at the Grecco School of Karate.

1

It was a big place, with large safety mats all around on the floor. That way, you wouldn't get hurt if you fell. One wall was covered with mirrors. Jonathan liked this because he could watch himself during practice.

He also liked the Asian pictures that hung on one wall. They made the school look like a real *dojo*. That was the Japanese word for "school."

Many kids came to the school. Some were as young as five, others were teenagers.

Jonathan and Susan were ten and a half, and Willy had just turned ten.

They all wore white uniforms, called *gis* ("gees"). The pants were baggy. The jacket had no buttons, and it was closed by a cloth belt. The belts came in different colors. They showed how good a person was at karate. Jonathan and his friends were blue belts. That was the second level.

"The camera zooms in for a close-up." Jonathan moved his hands up to Willy's face. "Cut!" he said. "That's how you make a movie."

"Is that all you think about?" Marissa asked.

Marissa Santos was nine. She had dark-brown hair and skin the color of light almonds.

Matthew Davis was next to her. He was nine and a half. His black hair was cut flat on top and short at the back and sides.

Jonathan grinned. "It's hard not to think about it. My parents bought me something awesome!"

Matthew gave Willy a high five. He turned to Jonathan. "Okay, Richie Rich," he said. "What did they buy you this week?"

"A terrific new Super-Zoom Hi-8 video camera," Jonathan said. "It zooms in close enough to see the label on a fly's jeans."

Matthew made a face. Then he moved his feet apart and stood with his back straight. He checked his balance by leaning left, then right.

"My new video camera is the best you can buy," Jonathan went on. "It has a supersensitive microphone. Date and time coding. Built-in editing features. It's great!"

"We know, Jonathan," Susan said. "You've been talking about it all day."

Matthew tucked his elbows in and clenched his fist. "You can talk all you want."

He began snapping punches at an imaginary opponent. "But me, I've got other things to do." *Snap*. "The Junior League Karate Contest is next week." *Snap*. "And we aren't ready."

"Why are you worried?" Jonathan asked. He looked around the dojo at the other students. Kids were stretching and practicing karate moves.

"We go to the best karate school in the city," Jonathan said. "I know because — "

"Your parents checked it out before they brought you here," Marissa said to Jonathan. "You told us that before."

"A hundred times," said Matthew. *Snap.*

Jonathan shrugged. "Well, it's true. My mother must have called every dojo in the book."

"Not my mother," Susan said quietly. "She saw some ad in the paper."

"Are you sorry?" Marissa asked. She and Susan liked each other, but they weren't best friends.

"I guess not." Susan stood in front of the mirrors fixing her hair.

Marissa leaned in close to Willy. She whispered, "Susan's really uptight lately."

"What's wrong with her?" Willy asked.

"I don't know," Marissa replied.

"Well, this is the best school," Jonathan said.

"Yeah," Matthew said. "It's cool!"

"We should call it the Cool Karate School!" Marissa said.

"Right," Jonathan said. "We'll win the karate contest hands down."

Matthew shook his head. "You think so?"

"Sure," Jonathan replied.

"Well, watch this," Matthew said.

He turned to Marissa. "Help me out. I want to try that jumping front kick we learned last week."

"Okay," Marissa replied.

Marissa and Matthew stood facing each other. They bowed, then began circling.

They exchanged moves. Marissa shot out a front punch and a reverse punch at Matthew's chest. Matthew stepped aside to avoid one. He used a side-arm block to stop the other.

They moved left, right, left, striking and blocking as they circled.

Jonathan glanced over at the teachers. The kids couldn't practice without supervision.

Punch, block, kick. Matthew and Marissa seemed to be evenly matched.

Willy was about to call it a tie when Matthew

leaped into the air. He tried to do a jumping front kick above Marissa's head.

But Marissa ducked under his leg and pushed it as it went by.

Matthew felt his balance go. He flopped on his back with a loud *whump*.

CHAPTER

NEAT
NICKNAMES

Matthew lay on the mat.

"Nice move, Snake," Susan said. Snake was Matthew's nickname.

In karate, the snake is flexible, graceful, and strong. Sometimes Matthew saw himself like that. He didn't feel that way now.

"Big joke." Matthew sighed. "I can't seem to keep up my defense."

"The Leopard can," Susan said. *"Aaaa!"*

Susan leaped into the air. She kicked out in front of her. Then she landed on her feet like a cat. "My jumping front kick is in great shape too."

Leopard was Susan's nickname. A leopard has speed and power. Susan was definitely a leopard.

"Well, excuse me for breathing," Marissa said.

8

Her nickname was Dragon. The dragon is the symbol for fighting spirit.

"Strength!" Jonathan took a step back. He stepped forward to deliver a front punch. "The Tiger is as strong as ever."

"The Tiger is also stubborn," Marissa said.

Jonathan grinned. "But I'm in top form."

"Your form's not bad," Willy said. "But that's not all we're doing in the contest. We have to spar with kids from other dojos."

"Spar" meant pretending to fight. You blocked kicks and punches. And you threw a few of your own. You weren't supposed to hit anybody.

Jonathan put his arm around Willy's shoulder. "Come on, Willy. You're the Crane," he said. "That means you've got grace and balance."

"Only sometimes," Willy grumbled.

"Willy is right," Matthew said. He got up from the floor and adjusted his gi. "We should be worried. I hear some of these kids are *baaaad!* "

"If they're so bad, what have we got to worry about?" Jonathan asked seriously.

"Sometimes," Susan said, "you're such a geek."

"Matthew meant that those kids are tough," Willy explained. "So we should practice more."

Marissa looked at Susan. "Even if some of us do think we're perfect."

Susan began doing her stretching exercises. First her legs, then her arms.

"All right, everyone. It's that time again," Tommy Grecco announced.

Just about every kid in the dojo liked Tommy. He was their *sensei* ("sen-say"), their teacher.

Tommy was a friendly-looking man with broad shoulders and brown hair. He was tall and strong. His movements were quick.

He never tried to make the kids feel afraid of him. He was always calm and patient. Even when they didn't do something right.

The kids formed three rows in front of Tommy. Then Su Grecco, Tommy's wife, came out.

Su was from Vietnam. She was also their teacher and an expert in karate. She was slender, with short black hair and bright-green eyes.

She smiled as she stood next to Tommy.

The teachers and the kids bowed to one another. Tommy signaled, and the kids sat down.

Jonathan closed his eyes. The room grew quiet. This was focusing time. The time when people cleared their minds of everything but karate.

Su told the kids to breathe in, then let the air out slowly. The breathing helped them push thoughts from their minds.

Marissa pushed away thoughts of her bullying older brothers. And a big, juicy cheeseburger.

Willy pushed away his father saying, "Win, win, win."

Susan let go of her anger toward her parents. Mr. and Mrs. Ziegler had been fighting over her lately, and Susan wasn't happy about it.

Matthew let go of the thought that the toughest kid on his block was looking for him. The kid hadn't liked the joke Matthew had played on him.

Jonathan forgot all about horseback riding last weekend. He took a breath. He pushed away thoughts of tennis. And the new CDs he had bought. He let out a breath.

But he couldn't forget about his new Super-Zoom video camera. He saw himself directing a big action movie.

With every breath he took, Jonathan could hear himself giving orders:

"Lights!" Breathe.

"Camera!" Breathe.

"Action!" Breathe.

Jonathan was behind the camera, telling everyone what to do. It was pure excitement.

"Whenever you're ready to join us, Mr. Scott." Tommy's voice broke into Jonathan's daydream.

Jonathan opened his eyes and saw the whole class was standing. Tommy was kneeling in front of him. "Are you ready?"

"Yes, sir." Jonathan stood up.

"That would be nice." Tommy jumped to his feet. He began to call out the Japanese names for karate forms.

Forms were groups of moves. They were like the movements of five animals: the tiger, snake, leopard, crane, and dragon.

The whole class moved together, doing the exercises. Jonathan watched himself in the mirror. He could see Susan too.

But he could tell the class wasn't doing everything right. Some kids' arms were too high. Or their feet were too far apart.

Jonathan glanced over at Matthew and Marissa. He could tell what they were thinking.

They were afraid the Junior League Karate Contest would turn into the Tournament of Doom.

CHAPTER
3

"LIGHTS, CAMERA... WATCH OUT!"

After class, Tommy and Su always gave the kids a cool-down period. Quiet time.

The students would do more deep breathing to help calm them. It also helped them to think about the lesson that day.

Sometimes Tommy would talk to them about the history of karate. Sometimes Su would talk about Asian history or her life in Vietnam.

Both teachers would talk about the "way of karate," the ideas behind it.

Jonathan and his friends loved this time.

"You don't study karate so you can break a board with your forehead," Tommy said. "Or so you can punch out the kid next door."

"That's why I started taking karate," Matthew

whispered to Marissa.

"If you'd stop playing tricks on people, you wouldn't need to fight anyone," Marissa said.

"Karate is a form of exercise for the body," Tommy was saying. "And for the mind."

"What if someone tries to pick a fight with us?" a boy called out from the last row.

"Yeah," said another boy. "Someone is always saying 'So you know karate, huh? Show me!'"

"You do not have to prove you know karate," Su told the class. "You do not have to fight to prove you know anything. You know what you know."

A new girl raised her hand. "But isn't fighting all we're going to learn in class?"

Tommy shook his head. "If that's all you learn," he said, "I haven't done my job." He stood up.

"The last thing I'll mention is the karate contest next week."

The kids started whispering.

"This is going to be great."

"I thought we had more time."

"Maybe I'll be sick next week."

Tommy signaled for everyone to calm down. "I just wanted to say that I've talked to the instructors at the other karate schools. We're all looking forward to a great event. We want you to have fun. And we want you to learn all you can."

"It'll be fun if we win," Willy said.

"Is that what you think?" Su asked.

"It's what my dad thinks, for sure."

Tommy and Su looked at each other.

"That's it for today," Tommy announced. "Go clean up and change. Your parents will be here in a few minutes."

Jonathan and his friends watched as the other kids hurried to the locker rooms.

"Tommy sure made us work hard," Susan said.

"We need it," Matthew said.

"Speak for yourself," Susan said. "I was fine."

"I don't know," Willy said. "The class looked sloppy to me."

"He's right," Matthew said. "My jumping front kick wasn't any better."

"Or my roundhouse kick," Marissa said.

Willy shook his head. "My dad's going to be mad if I don't bring home a trophy."

"I can't wait," Jonathan said. "Maybe my dad will tape it. If he comes." He stared at the floor.

"Your folks will be there," Willy said. "Everybody's folks are coming."

"Don't bet on it," Susan said, shaking out her frizzy hair.

"The problem is we need more practice time," Willy said. "We have to figure out what we're doing wrong."

"What do you mean, 'we'?" Susan asked.

Jonathan threw his arm around Marissa. "I don't see what the problem is," he said. "Tommy and Su aren't worried."

"Maybe they didn't notice our mistakes," Willy said. "There are ten other kids in the class."

"Look. We're the best." Jonathan tried a side kick. He slipped and fell.

"That doesn't count," he said. "Let's forget about the contest and talk about my camera. I have a great movie idea."

"I have a better idea," Matthew said. "Let's have Jonathan videotape our karate workouts."

Willy snapped his fingers. "Right! That way we can see what we're doing wrong! And we can fix it before the contest!"

"That is a super idea!" Jonathan said. "I can practice on you. Then I'll be an expert when I shoot my real movie."

"I don't know," Marissa said. "Cameras make you look ten pounds heavier."

"Losing the contest won't make us look too good either," said Matthew.

"I say we give it a try!" Willy said. "What about you, Susan?"

Susan looked bored. "Why not?"

"All right, then," Jonathan said. "I'll ask Tommy if it's okay. I know he'll say yes." He dashed across the room.

Jonathan shouted over his shoulder. "Tomorrow it will be lights, camera — "

"Watch out!" Willy shouted.

Jonathan plowed into a man who was carrying a

stack of papers as he entered the room.

Jonathan and the man fell to the floor in a heap. The flyers the man was carrying flew up into the air. Jonathan and the man seemed to be trapped in a storm of giant snowflakes.

CHAPTER

GETTING PERMISSION

Tommy hurried over to the man. Soon they were laughing about the accident.

Willy, Susan, and the others helped Jonathan pick up the flyers. Then Jonathan went over to talk with Tommy.

Later, Jonathan told his parents about taping the class. "Tommy said I could!" Jonathan said.

"That's fine, dear," said Jonathan's mother. She was in the front of the car with Jonathan's father. She was reading papers from her briefcase.

Jonathan was in the back. He liked the drive home. It was one of the few times he got to see both his parents at once.

Jonathan's parents were always busy. Mrs. Scott

worked for a big advertising agency. She wrote commercials.

"Tommy said I could start shooting Thursday," Jonathan went on. "So can I — "

"May I," Mr. Scott said.

Mr. Scott owned a company that helped movie and recording stars with their businesses.

Jonathan had been on the sets of many movies.

"May I take my camera to karate class?"

"Who will be responsible for it?" his father asked. "And how will you practice if you are holding the camera?"

Jonathan was used to his father's questions.

"I'm only taping my friends, Willy, Matthew, Susan, and Marissa," he said. "We're getting there early, before the rest of the class."

His father's cell phone rang.

Jonathan hated it when his parents got phone calls. They even brought a phone with them on vacation.

Jonathan looked out the window. They were

close to their apartment.

Mr. Scott hung up the phone. "Will you be videotaping the whole class?" he asked.

He forgot what I said, Jonathan thought. "Just my friends."

"If you promise to be careful, I guess it will be all right," Mrs. Scott said. "I'll take the camera to work with me. When I drop you off at class, I'll bring it along."

"Great!" said Jonathan. Then he remembered the contest. He still didn't know if his parents were coming. "Are you guys —"

"Guys?" His father raised an eyebrow.

"Are you and Mom going to—" A cell phone rang again. This time it was for his mother. She spoke quickly and hung up.

Jonathan tried again. "Are you and Mom — "

"We're at the garage," his father said. "Let's park the car, and we'll talk upstairs."

But the phone rang the minute they walked into the apartment. Jonathan went to his room.

From the window, he looked down at the big park across the street. He could also see the river beyond the park.

The sun was setting. Orange, red, and purple.

Nice shot, he thought.

Jonathan flopped down on the bed.

What if his parents couldn't come to the contest? He could tape it. Show it to them later.

Maybe.

If they had time.

CHAPTER

5

MR. HOLLYWOOD

Thursday was damp and chilly.

Jonathan's mother dropped him off at the dojo a half hour early.

Tommy and Su were happy to see him.

"We'll keep an eye on his equipment," Tommy told Mrs. Scott. She kissed Jonathan good-bye and said she'd be back in two hours.

"Your friends haven't arrived yet," Su told Jonathan. "But you can set up the camera in the corner."

Tommy helped Jonathan carry his equipment. Jonathan held the camera and his karate uniform. Tommy took the tripod and a big shoulder bag.

"I brought a lot of tapes," Jonathan said, pointing at the bag. "I don't want to miss a thing."

He began to set up the tripod. He pulled out the skinny legs until they were the right length. Then he tightened them and attached the camera.

The other kids arrived. Marissa, Willy, and Matthew looked cheerful. But Susan still seemed to be in a bad mood.

Jonathan was too excited to care. "Let's change fast," he said. "We've only got a half hour before the class gets here."

They headed for the locker rooms. "I've got a feeling this isn't going to be fun," Matthew said.

A few minutes later, Jonathan and Matthew came out of the locker room. Willy, Marissa, and Susan were waiting.

"No way!" Matthew shouted.

"But it would be a great way to start the movie!" Jonathan said.

"Forget it!"

"What's wrong?" Susan asked.

Matthew made a sour face. "Jonathan wants to tape us changing in the lockers."

"But it would have been cool," Jonathan told

the others. "Matthew had on these funny boxer shorts —"

Matthew clamped his hand over Jonathan's mouth. Willy, Marissa, and Susan giggled.

"Let's just get this movie going," Matthew said. "All right?"

Jonathan had the gang start the workout. First they warmed up by doing stretches. Then they did their exercises together.

Jonathan and his camera were everywhere. He knelt by Marissa and aimed at her face.

"Don't shoot up my nose," she told him.

Other students began to arrive at the dojo. They came over to watch. Some of them even started posing for the camera. But Jonathan stayed focused on the gang.

Jonathan ran alongside Willy as he did a series of kicks. Willy stumbled.

"I got that shot," Jonathan said, smiling.

"Terrific," Willy grunted.

Jonathan stood in front of Susan. She threw punches and blocks.

Then they practiced sparring. Jonathan lay on the mat. He got a great shot of Matthew, who did his jumping front kick. But Matthew slipped and fell on the mat.

"Got to work on that," Jonathan told Matthew. Matthew frowned.

Jonathan took a lot of shots of Susan. When he did, her shouts became louder. And her moves became wilder.

"Great action," he told her.

Sometimes he didn't get the shot he wanted. So Jonathan would make her do it again and again.

He was having a great time.

His friends were not.

"I'm not doing another thing. I don't care what you say," Marissa groaned.

"Me either." Willy rubbed his legs.

"The class hasn't even started and I'm already tired," Matthew said.

"I just want this to look like a real movie," Jonathan told them. "I'm going to call it *The Cool Karate School.*"

"We're not making a movie, Mr. Hollywood," Marissa said. "We're doing this so we can do better in the contest."

"And you haven't been practicing," Willy said.

Jonathan put a new tape in the camera. "I told you, I'm ready for the contest. So is Susan."

Marissa let out a deep sigh. "Let's look at the tape and see."

"Okay," Jonathan said. "We can watch it in the viewfinder."

The kids gathered around the camera.

They were not happy with what they saw.

Willy turned away when he saw himself fall.

Marissa didn't like her form.

Matthew thought he was dopey-looking.

"Great, huh?" said Jonathan. Willy rolled his eyes. Matthew grumbled.

"Let's go, people," Tommy said. "We've got a lot to do."

"I guess we can watch this again later," Willy suggested.

"Gee, I can't wait," Marissa said.

Matthew, Willy, and Marissa hurried over to join the class.

Susan stayed long enough to help Jonathan put the equipment against the wall.

"You looked good on tape," Jonathan told her. "You'll be great in the contest."

Susan smiled. "Thanks."

"Are your parents coming to see you?"

Susan's eyes narrowed. "I don't know." She started to walk away.

"I don't know if mine are coming either," Jonathan told her.

Susan turned and looked at him.

"They're pretty busy," he told her. "Is that why yours aren't coming?"

"Kind of," Susan said. Her shoulders sagged. "I don't know."

Tommy called to them. Susan and Jonathan ran over to join the class.

Jonathan took his place in line. He hoped his parents would come.

He hoped Susan's parents would be there too.

CHAPTER

ARE WE READY FOR THIS?

The kids had a good class. Tommy and Su went over the rules of the contest. They also told the kids how to act when they met the other schools.

Matthew said Tommy should teach them the rules of first aid.

Susan poked him in the side.

Then Su talked to them about attitude.

"You are not going into this contest to hurt people," she said. "It is not a match to see who is tougher. Or who is stronger."

"Then how can we beat them?" a girl asked.

"This contest is not about beating," Tommy said. His voice was gentle, but he looked very serious.

"You were a soldier once," Jonathan said.

33

"Didn't you have to fight?"

Tommy and Su glanced at each other.

"Yes, I was a soldier once," Tommy said. "And I had to fight a war in Su's country.

"But that is where I learned an important lesson. Fighting is hard on everybody. Learning how not to fight is harder."

"Then why learn karate?" Susan asked.

"We learn the *art* of karate," Tommy said. He jumped up and began to perform a series of moves.

He looks like a dancer, Jonathan thought.

Tommy's moves were quick and strong.

He kicked his leg high over his head and held it there for a moment. He slowly fell to the floor. Then he rose up and glided across the room.

He stopped and stood without moving. He took deep breaths, then let them out as he moved again.

Jonathan and his friends watched with wide eyes. They knew many karate forms were based on the movements of animals. They could see some of those animals in Tommy's movements.

"That is the art of karate," Su told them. "When you put winning over the art, you lose everything."

When cool-down time was over, the parents began to arrive.

Jonathan was next to Willy. He heard Willy's father telling his son he had to win a trophy. "I guess Mr. Ray doesn't know much about the art of karate," Jonathan whispered to Marissa.

"He's sure making it hard on Willy." Marissa was staring at Susan's T-shirt. It had flowers wearing leather jackets on it.

Willy came over to his friends. "I was just thinking ..."

Matthew grinned. "Tell us quickly before you forget!"

"I know we looked dumb on the tape. But we were pretty good in class today."

"So?" Susan asked.

"I say we stop worrying and give it our best shot."

Marissa's eyes brightened. "Why not?" she

said. "My whole family's coming. I'd better be good."

"I'm game," Matthew said. "High five!"

Marissa, Willy, Susan, and Matthew all slapped hands in the air.

Jonathan was holding the camera. It was the first time his friends were feeling good about the match. Why didn't he?

He felt his father's arm drop around his shoulder. Mr. Scott squeezed playfully.

"Are you ready to go?" he asked Jonathan.

"Sure thing." Jonathan turned to pick up the rest of his video equipment.

"I'll see you children at the contest on Thursday," Mr. Scott said.

"You mean you're coming?" Jonathan cried.

"Of course," said Mr. Scott. "Your mother and I wouldn't miss it."

Jonathan jumped in the air. He ran over to his friends and gave them all a big high five.

"To the contest!" he cheered.

"Let's do it!" the gang shouted.

CHAPTER 7

THE TOURNAMENT OF DOOM

Over the weekend Jonathan replayed the tapes.

Something bothered him. But he couldn't figure out what.

On Tuesday he tried to take a few more shots. But Marissa, Willy, and Matthew weren't interested. They wanted to practice.

Only Susan was willing. Jonathan shot some footage of her. Then she became bored.

Before the class ended, Su said, "We'll meet at the Carter Gym on Thursday at four o'clock."

When Jonathan left with his mother, the room was buzzing. Everybody was talking about the contest. Jonathan knew the class could hardly wait. And neither could he.

Jonathan and his parents arrived for the contest

on time. His parents were never late for anything.

Jonathan's stomach felt funny when he saw the gymnasium. It was huge. Bigger than the one in Jonathan's school. Against two walls, there were benches filled with people.

Four dojos were competing in the match. A banner was taped on the wall over each group.

Jonathan's parents took seats in the bleachers. Jonathan joined his friends.

"There must be a zillion kids here," he said.

Susan was walking back and forth. She kept playing with a strand of her hair.

"Are you nervous?" Jonathan asked her.

"Believe it."

"Me too," Jonathan said.

"I thought you two had it all under control," Marissa said.

"I didn't know there would be so many people," Jonathan said.

Matthew's and Marissa's parents were sitting together. Matthew's mom was fiddling with a camera.

Marissa waved to her mother. "My family is over there," she said.

Jonathan spotted Willy's father, Mr. Ray. He was sitting with four other men. All of them wore jackets that said "Ray's Construction Company." Willy's father built houses.

"Isn't that your mom and dad sitting with my parents?" Jonathan asked Susan.

Susan tried to smile. "Yeah," she said. "My dad didn't want to come, but he changed his mind."

"Is something wrong?" Marissa asked.

"My folks have been arguing a lot," Susan said.

Tommy called to the group. "This is it, people," he said. "It's time to change."

"Don't worry about anything," Su said. "Remember, we're here to have fun and to learn."

A voice cried out from the bleachers. "Win us a trophy, son!"

It was Mr. Ray. He and his friends cheered.

"I want to throw up," Willy said.

"Save it for the match," Marissa told him. "We may need a secret weapon."

When the kids returned from the lockers, the other teams were ready.

Three judges sat at one end of the gym. Mats lay on the floor, and there was a referee.

Su led the kids in a brief period of focus time. Then Tommy spoke to them.

"Remember, you get one point for each good kick or punch. You must do the move right, and you must be in control. You have to be in the 'target area' — above the waist. And always aim for the front of the body, not the back."

"Don't forget, you can't actually hit anyone," Su added. "This is not a contact sport."

"Three points wins, right?" Jonathan asked.

"Right," said Tommy. "But just think about doing your best."

The judges called for the contest to begin.

The teams took their turns bowing to the judges. This was to show respect.

Then each team performed an exhibition of their forms.

The team with green uniforms went first.

"They're good," Willy said.

"They don't worry me," Matthew said.

The next team wore black uniforms. Their form looked almost perfect.

And the third team wore black and white gis. The crowd cheered when they finished.

Matthew swallowed hard. "*They* worry me."

Finally it was time for Jonathan and his team. Jonathan couldn't concentrate.

And he started worrying about weird things: Were their white uniforms clean enough? Did their voices sound squeaky?

When they had finished, he wasn't sure how well they had done.

The judges wrote on their note pads.

Next, each team picked who would spar with whom on the other teams. They had to match opponents by size, age, and skill.

Jonathan, Susan, and two other kids from their dojo were chosen to spar first.

"Don't worry," Jonathan said. "We're the best." He waved to his father, who was holding the video camera ready.

Tommy walked Jonathan over to the mat. He gave him some instructions, then stepped back.

Jonathan bowed to his opponent. He was a thin boy in a black and white gi.

They both bowed to the judges.

The referee gave the start command. Jonathan felt his stomach jump.

The next thing that jumped was the boy.

He came at Jonathan all hands and feet.

Jonathan knew he didn't have a chance.

AND THE
WINNERS ARE...

The boy never hit Jonathan. He stopped his punches just inches away. But he was gaining points. Jonathan was in trouble.

Jonathan blocked a few of the boy's moves. But he scored only one point before time ran out.

Jonathan felt like a dope. He had thought he was so cool. Now he knew he wasn't.

He knew he'd lost before he heard the score. He could tell by the looks on his friends' faces.

"I blew it," he said when he joined the others.

"Don't worry about it," Marissa said.

"I thought you'd be mad at me," Jonathan said. "Especially after the way I bragged."

"You're a jerk sometimes," Marissa said. "But we're a team. And we're friends."

It was Susan's turn.

"She looks even more nervous than Jonathan," Willy whispered.

Matthew leaned forward to get a better view. "Cross your fingers, guys."

Susan's match was shorter than Jonathan's. Her opponent scored the three winning points in a few minutes.

When the match was over, Susan looked like she was going to cry.

"It's cool," Matthew told her when she returned. "The contest isn't over yet."

"But I lost my match." Susan dropped down onto the floor and crossed her legs.

"Then you'd better cheer real loud," Willy told her. "Because the rest of us have to go out there and try."

"Cheer hard for me," Matthew said. "I want my folks to think I have a lot of fans."

The match was exciting. Jonathan and his friends saw some kids perform moves their team couldn't. Other kids weren't as good as the kids from the Cool Karate School.

But all the kids seemed to be doing their best.

Willy's match was a tie.

Matthew's jumping front kick got him the winning point.

Marissa did the best in her age group.

But when the scores were finally announced, the Grecco Karate School took third place.

"We lost!" said Jonathan.

"They beat us into the ground." Matthew stamped his foot.

"And it's all my fault," Jonathan said.

"Mine too," said Susan. "We should have spent more time practicing. Then we might have won!"

"Tommy and Su are going to hate me," said Jonathan.

"And your dad got it all on tape," Marissa said.

Jonathan lowered his head. "Oh, great. Here comes Tommy."

"Good work!" he cried.

"Good?" Matthew was confused. "We lost!"

"Why do you think that?" Tommy asked.

"We came in last," said Susan.

"Third place," Tommy corrected her.

"Okay. Next to last. That's just as bad."

"Don't you remember what Su and I told you?" The kids looked confused.

"First of all, you entered the contest. That alone makes you a winner. Many people never make that first step."

The gang looked at one another.

"Second," Tommy said, "you did your best. I can't ask for more than that. Remember, it's the art of karate you're learning."

"But I really wanted to win something," Jonathan said.

"Did you? Think about it," Tommy said. "Wasn't there something even more important?"

Jonathan thought hard. "I wanted my parents to come see me," he said.

"And they came, didn't they?" Tommy asked.

"Yeah." Jonathan looked at Susan.

She wrinkled up her face. Then she sighed and grinned too. "Yes, I'm glad my parents came too.

My dad wanted me to take ballet. He didn't want me to learn karate. 'It isn't right for a girl,' he said. But my mom kept arguing that it was."

"Is that why you've been such a grouch?" Marissa asked.

"Was I that bad?"

"How about total pain?"

The two girls laughed.

"The important things are usually the simple ones," Tommy told them.

"Try telling that to my dad," Willy said.

"I just did," Tommy said. "I think he understood."

Willy looked over at his father. He was smiling.

Jonathan's father came hurrying over to the group.

"That was an excellent match," he said. "I have it all on tape. Every thrilling moment."

"Did I look fat?" Marissa asked.

"No, you did not, young lady," said Mr. Scott. He spoke very fast. "You looked super. You all did." He pointed Jonathan's new video camera at

Tommy and the gang.

"Now I'd like to get some behind-the-scenes footage," he said.

Jonathan frowned. "Dad, I think —"

"Just a minute, son." He closed one eye and looked through the viewfinder. "It looks dark. I hope there's enough light."

"But, Dad, I — "

"Just act natural."

"Dad!" Jonathan called out.

Mr. Scott frowned. "You don't have to shout, Jonathan."

"Sorry. But the camera works better if you take the lens cap off."

Mr. Scott pulled off the cap. "Oh, no! I hope I took that off before the match."

"That's all right," Jonathan said. "Some things are better live and in person!" He gave his father a hug.

"There's a rumor about food back at our dojo," Tommy said. "Juice, fruit, and pizzas!"

"Sounds like a party to me!" Matthew said.

The gang leaped into the air.

"Let's do it!" they shouted, and ran for the door.

This is Steve DeMasco, creator of the Cool Karate School books, and five of his students.

Steve has a seventh-degree black belt in karate. That means he's one of the best karate experts in the world. He has appeared in movies and is the star of a self-defense videotape.

Steve believes kids can learn good values from karate— and have a lot of fun too.

These kids are just starting out, but they're doing great. They really get a kick out of karate—just like the kids of the Cool Karate School!